# Li'l Rabbit's KWANZAA

Donna L. Washington     Illustrated by Shane W. Evans

 KATHERINE TEGEN BOOKS
An Imprint of HarperCollins Publishers

Li'l Rabbit was not having a very good Kwanzaa. Being the littlest rabbit in the family wasn't easy.

He couldn't remember the names of all the days. He wasn't allowed to light the candles. His brothers and sisters made wonderful gifts to share. Li'l Rabbit was too embarrassed to share his gifts. He hated being the youngest. He was always in the way and everyone told him he was too little to help.

The only part of Kwanzaa that he really loved was the big feast called Karamu. This year, he wasn't even going to have that. Granna Rabbit was sick. She lay in bed all day drinking dandelion tea. Momma Rabbit was so busy taking care of her, she didn't have time to cook.

"Momma, if Granna Rabbit is sick, who will make the feast of Karamu?" Li'l Rabbit asked his mother.

"Shame on you, Li'l Rabbit," his momma said. "Granna Rabbit is sick and all you think about is your stomach. You go outside."

Li'l Rabbit hopped out and sat on the big, gnarled tree stump. He really wanted to go and talk to Granna Rabbit. She was very wise.

Li'l Rabbit sat and thought. He thought about all the things his granna said about Kwanzaa.

"Kwanzaa is a special time when we help each other." That's what Granna Rabbit said.

"That's it!" Li'l Rabbit jumped up and danced around. "I'll bring Granna Rabbit a special treat for Karamu. That will make her feel better."

Li'l Rabbit hopped down the road. "Where are you going so fast?" Momma Oriole asked Li'l Rabbit.

"I'm going to find a tasty treat for Granna Rabbit. She's sick. I want her to have a good Karamu." Li'l Rabbit hopped away.

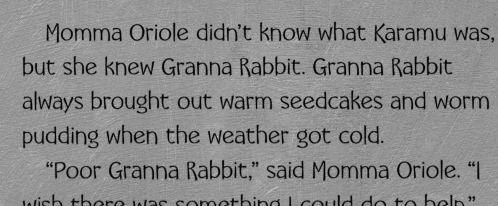

Momma Oriole didn't know what Karamu was, but she knew Granna Rabbit. Granna Rabbit always brought out warm seedcakes and worm pudding when the weather got cold.

"Poor Granna Rabbit," said Momma Oriole. "I wish there was something I could do to help."

Li'l Rabbit stopped by the side of the path. He looked under some logs to see if he could find something special for Granna Rabbit.

"What are you doing, Li'l Rabbit?" asked Groundhog, sticking his head out of a patch of grass.

"I'm trying to find a Zawadi for Granna Rabbit. She's sick. I want her to feel better." Li'l Rabbit hopped off.

Groundhog didn't know what a Zawadi was, but he knew Granna Rabbit. She always had time to make little toys for the animals when they were bored.

"Poor Granna Rabbit," said Groundhog. "I wish there was something I could do to help."

Li'l Rabbit hopped down to the pond. Maybe he could find something pretty for Granna Rabbit.

"What are you doing, Li'l Rabbit?" asked the frogs.

"I'm looking for something pretty for Granna Rabbit. She's sick. She should have something pretty to hang on the wall at Kwanzaa time." Li'l Rabbit scratched an ear and hopped away.

The frogs didn't know anything
about Kwanzaa time, but they knew
Granna Rabbit. She could paint beautiful
pictures and write wonderful poems.
   "Poor Granna Rabbit," said one of the frogs.
"I wish there was something we could do to help."

Li'l Rabbit hopped through the field looking for berries.

"Where are you going, Li'l Rabbit?" Momma Field Mouse asked. She was dragging all of her children behind her.

"Granna Rabbit is sick," said Li'l Rabbit. "I'm going to make sure she has a good Karamu. I'm going to find as many berries as I can." Li'l Rabbit looked proud as he hopped through the meadow.

Momma Field Mouse didn't know anything about Karamu, but she knew Granna Rabbit. Granna Rabbit helped out with the children when Momma Field Mouse had to run errands.

"Poor Granna Rabbit," said Momma Field Mouse. "I wish there was something I could do to help."

Li'l Rabbit scampered through the trees.

"Good morning, Li'l Rabbit," said Poppa Squirrel. "Why are you sniffing around the trees?"

Best Trees to climb
By Warren Walnut

"I'm looking for something to give Granna Rabbit. She's sick. I want her to have a good Kwanzaa." Li'l Rabbit hopped away.

Poppa Squirrel didn't know anything about Kwanzaa, but he knew Granna Rabbit. She always helped him gather nuts in the fall. She even helped him remember where he hid them.

"Poor Granna Rabbit," said Poppa Squirrel. "I wish there was something I could do to help."

Li'l Rabbit spent the whole day trying to find something for Granna Rabbit. He searched as hard as he could, but he didn't find anything at all. He was very sad.

"I guess I am too little to do anything."

As the sun was setting, he hopped slowly home. When he opened the door, he had a big surprise.

Everyone was there! Granna Rabbit was sitting in the big chair with a huge smile on her face. The frogs had brought pink flowers from the lily pads. Momma and Poppa Spider hung them from the ceiling like lanterns. Momma Oriole was conducting a fine chorus of birds.

Groundhog brought little toys and gifts for everyone. Momma Field Mouse had gotten together with Momma Possum and Momma Raccoon to make a delicious feast. The air was full of excitement. Momma Rabbit served the plates, and Li'l Rabbit ate until he thought he would burst.

After that, Poppa Rabbit told funny stories about Brer Rabbit, Anansi the Spider, Guinea Fowl, and Mosquito. The stories made everyone laugh. Then, Poppa Spider plucked on his web strings, Cricket got out his fiddle, and all the animals had a wonderful dance.

Granna Rabbit taught everyone a new word.
"Harambee!" she called out as her friends danced.
"It means 'Let's pull together!'"
"We don't need anyone to tell us that!" said Poppa
Squirrel. "We already pulled together!"
Everyone laughed and shouted,
"Harambee! Harambee! Harambee!"

# The Nguzo Saba–
## The Seven Principles of Kwanzaa

Day 1. Umoja – Unity
The animals joined together to celebrate Karamu.

Day 2. Kujichagulia – Self-determination
Li'l Rabbit began his search all on his own.

Day 3. Ujima – Working Together
Momma Field Mouse, Momma Possum, and
Momma Raccoon worked to make the feast.
The frogs and spiders hung the lanterns.
Spider and Cricket made the music.

Day 4. Ujamaa – Supporting each other in business
Granna Rabbit helps Poppa Squirrel hide his nuts and
find them again in the spring. Granna Rabbit helps
Momma Field Mouse with her children.

### Day 5. Nia – Purpose

Li'l Rabbit left home with a purpose. He wanted to help his granna have a wonderful Karamu.

### Day 6. Kuumbaa – Creativity

The storytelling, dancing, music, painting, poetry, making the Zawadi for the party, and cooking are examples of creativity.

**Karamu** – The Feast of Kwanzaa happens the sixth night of Kwanzaa.

### Day 7. Imani – Faith

Granna Rabbit has faith in Li'l Rabbit.

**Zawadi** – Presents you give at Kwanzaa. Many of them are handmade. Groundhog brought handmade toys and gifts to the Karamu.

## Can you find other examples of the Nguzo Saba in the story?

For my mother, Gwendolyn Washington, aka Granna, and all of her Li'l Rabbits:
Jaslyn, Devin, Darith, Don Mutaba, Darren Kalenga, Zolynn, and Lourdes.
—D.L.W.


Thank you, God. This book is dedicated to Sister Tebogo and
Brother Buntu. Thank you for your gifts on what will be my most
memorable Kwanzaa celebration. Blessings, Tshegofatso.
—S.W.E.

Katherine Tegen Books is an imprint of HarperCollins Publishers.

Li'l Rabbit's Kwanzaa

Text copyright © 2010 by Donna L. Washington

Illustrations copyright © 2010 by Shane W. Evans

All rights reserved. Manufactured in China.

No part of this book may be used or reproduced in any manner whatsoever without written permission

except in the case of brief quotations embodied in critical articles and reviews. For information address

HarperCollins Children's Books, a division of HarperCollins Publishers, 10 East 53rd Street, New York, NY 10022.

www.harpercollinschildren.com

Library of Congress Cataloging-in-Publication Data

Washington, Donna L.

Li'l Rabbit's Kwanzaa / Donna L. Washington ; illustrated by Shane W. Evans. — 1st ed.

p.     cm.

Summary: Li'l Rabbit searches for a gift for his grandmother when she is sick during Kwanzaa, and surprises her with the best gift of all.

Includes the "Nguzo Saba—the Seven Principles of Kwanzaa."

ISBN 978-0-06-072816-8 (trade bdg.) — ISBN 978-0-06-072817-5 (lib. bdg.)

[1. Kwanzaa—Fiction.   2. Rabbits—Fiction. 3. Animals—Fiction.]   I. Evans, Shane, ill.   II. Title.   III. Title: Little Rabbit's Kwanzaa.

PZ7.W25854Li   2010     2009031223     [E]—dc22     CIP     AC

Typography by Rachel Zegar

10  11  12  13  14  SCP  10  9  8  7  6  5  4  3  2  1

❖

First Edition